Every Lady is a Woman
but Every Woman

Every Lady is a Woman,
but Every Woman is NOT a Lady

Every Lady is a Woman, But every Woman is NOT a Lady © 2015 by Essence K. Berry. All rights reserved. No part of this book may be reproduced or transmitted in any form or by any means, electronic or mechanical, including photocopying, recording, or by any information storage and retrieval system, without written permission from the copyright owner or the publisher.

Tobias Publishing
ISBN 978-0-9907488-1-6

Essence K. Berry

Every Lady is a Woman,
but Every Woman is NOT a Lady

For Shardonay Jones, for speaking my blessings into existence...

Every Lady is a Woman,
but Every Woman is NOT a Lady

The tale of a lady's submission to her inner beast

Essence K. Berry

Every Lady is a Woman,
but Every Woman is NOT a Lady

Dear Reader:

I hope you read and enjoyed my breakout work, "The Single Friend", which took you on an erotic journey through my life as a single woman, introducing you to some of my most fulfilling and memorable lovers. This book differs slightly, as I take you on an expedition of my conflicts with my public face versus the one I unleash behind closed doors.

Understand, I was raised in the true fashion of everything a young lady is expected to be. The women in my life trained, taught, and corrected unladylike behavior. It was essential to know how to brush my skirt underneath me before I took a seat; to be aware of a man's hand placement when he escorted and danced with me; and how to present myself publicly so as not to be mistaken for one of the "fast girls". It was drilled into me there were certain behaviors which were unacceptable for "good girls".

Essence K. Berry

Every Lady is a Woman,
but Every Woman is NOT a Lady

I dared to push the boundaries of socially acceptable behaviors, unleashing the sexual beast that resides in me as I quenched my insatiable thirst. As a result, I frequently disregarded the etiquette lessons I was taught, answering to the ferocious beastly callings instead.

That thirsty little beast, whose appetite never seemed to be satiated, was constantly on the prowl. With no success, I tried to tame the intuitive callings over the years; scolding the animalistic nature that lay just at the brink of escaping when a man's heavenly aroma graced my senses and stirred that wild thing in me. Eventually, I had to come to terms with what stares me in my face daily: I am a hell of a lady when I need to present that side to the world, but I do love to unbridle the beast that I attempt to sedate when the lady in me is present.

The impish ways of my little mischievous creature would be frowned upon by society's ladies. The flagrant

Every Lady is a Woman,
but Every Woman is NOT a Lady

sexual acts that please my little monster are unthinkable among "ladies" with proper upbringing. My beautiful brute lives for the nasty, she delights in the taboo, and she anxiously awaits a willing partner who will submit to her hot desires! She pokes her little head out and delights in those who have no idea that the mannerable lady before them is always on the hunt!

Please allow me to share a few of the candid tales of the times I released my ravenous beast to come out to play, forsaking the years of etiquette that were so carefully instilled in me. Sometimes the beast had to overtake the lady and command the scene until her sweet appetite was sated.....Happy reading my Sweet Berries!

-Essence K. Berry

*Every Lady is a Woman,
but Every Woman is NOT a Lady*

Prologue

Ladies, are you ever graced by your mother's voice at the most inopportune moments? I can often hear mine admonishing me about the importance of being a lady, just as I am about to allow my inner animal full control! When I relinquish control to the sexual creature that resides in me, I simply sit back and enjoy the ride. The exquisite fiendish being is charged with the task of feeding until her thirst is quenched. Whatever she *thinks* will feel good to me is acceptable to me. I allow her creative juices to flow until her desires come to fruition and my molten lava is flowing! My beast is bold, uninhibited, and knows how to drive me to a state of unequivocal ecstasy!

For generations, women have passed down essential advice to the next generation of young ladies to ensure the expectations of proper etiquette are understood. For example, how a lady should sit, walk, and eat; proper grooming habits; and how to conduct one's self in certain attire. I tried to stay on the right path, but occasionally I jumped off and ran along a wilder path; one less traveled and more adventurous. Enjoy the road less traveled ladies, as the thrill of the ride is astounding. Find your beast, release the reins, and enjoy! However, never, *never* forget your lessons in etiquette! Have fun!

Every Lady is a Woman,
but Every Woman is NOT a Lady

Essence:

"*The intrinsic nature or indispensable quality of something, especially something abstract that determines its character.*"

-Oxford

Presentation of the Lessons:

Lesson #1 "A lady does not wrestle or horse play!"

Lesson #2 "Ladies keep their dresses down!"

Lesson #3 "A lady never bends over; she carefully stoops."

Lesson #4: "A lady does not sweat; she glistens"

Lesson #5 "A lady is NEVER to drink from a bottle"

Lesson #6 "A lady always sits with her legs closed"

Lesson #7 "A lady is groomed at all times"

*Every Lady is a Woman,
but Every Woman is NOT a Lady*

Lesson #8 "A lady does not play with her food!"

Lesson #9 "Ladies do not lick their fingers!"

Lesson #10 "A lady is careful to conceal her undergarments"

Part One: The Observation

Part Two: Lights, Camera, Action

Every Lady is a Woman,
but Every Woman is NOT a Lady

Lesson #1: "A lady does not wrestle or horseplay!"

One minute we are on the sofa, having an unspoken battle for dominance over the armrest that separates us as we take in an afternoon movie, the next, there is a clear struggle to prove dominance. As I have never claimed to be much of a lady, it matters very little to me that I am supposed to be dainty and not so prone to desire control in this situation. The battle for power results in an exchange of fury from my eyes to his and a clear challenge is marked at this point. An arm wrestle ensues, and ends with me being tossed from the plush sofa onto the carpeted floor. The battle for submission is all that remains. Stubbornly, I refuse to relinquish control to him. I am not fazed by the fact that he does this for sport with guys who are bigger, stronger, and more skilled than myself. If he wants me to submit, he's going to have to make me and I do *not* plan to make it easy for him! I did listen when my mama told me to make a man work for it!

My hair is escaping its perfect ponytail and my carefully placed bangs are no longer masterfully outlining my face. My mom would be shaking her head in dismay at this scene unfolding, as young ladies do not behave in such a manner! I do nothing to maintain modesty as my shoulder escapes my tank top when my opponent pins me face down and pulls my elbows together behind my back. I manage to pull out of his grasp and land on my back with a thud! That one motion tosses the lady aside and sets my raging beast free!

No sooner than I make my breakaway, he lands on top of me and expertly pins my arms above my head and helps himself to a nip on my nipple. Wrapping my legs around his massive body, I squeeze with all my might until he releases my arms. Making note of his growing excitement, I take advantage of his distraction and begin to wiggle from underneath him.

Flipping me over so I am face down again, he captures me and puts his weight back on my body.

"Oh no you don't! Where do you think you're going?"

Slipping his arms underneath mine and locking his hands behind my head, I have nowhere to go! Arms up, face down, breasts thrust out, and I am his for the taking.

Submission. That was what it all boiled down to.

"Gotcha," he whispers into my ear.

"Mmm. Looks that way big boy. Congrats."

Hair a mess, clothes in disarray, and panting from the tussle, I await his next move, as I have come to enjoy our unorthodox matches and the reward that follows when he wins.

"Promise not to run?"

"Promise."

"Good, because I won. Say I won."

"I won."

"Oh, smart ass today, huh?"

He pulls my arms further back and positions himself deeper between my thighs. I can feel his solid erection threatening the seam of my shorts through his gym shorts.

"I said what you told me to say. Stop pulling! Yes, you win! Damn! Now let me up!"

"Or what?"

Just because he can, he releases me from the Full Nelson hold he has on me, but swiftly captures my arms, continuing to limit my range of motion and keeping me face down on the floor. Rolling me to the side just enough to slip a hand underneath my breast, he starts to knead a handful through my top. Daring to venture into the side of my tank top, he manipulates my hard nipple until I squirm appreciatively under his talented touch.

Every Lady is a Woman, but Every Woman is NOT a Lady

"Yeah, that's what I'm talking about. I'm still not letting you go though."

With that announcement, he shifts his weight to his knees, taking my wrists with him, and straddles my outstretched legs. Running his fingers along my shorts, he slips his finger past my panties and into my dampness.

"Ummm, wet already?"

He slides his fingers in and out of me, watching with satisfaction as I writhe and take the finger fucking. Tickling my clit before he withdraws his finger from my panties, I observe the calculated release of his manhood from his shorts.

"Are you going to let me go?"

"Nope. I won. Remember?"

Without bothering to remove my shorts or my panties, my opponent slides his body back down onto mine, grinds his erection between my thighs, and places me back into a Full Nelson hold. He uses his thighs to push mine further apart so I am completely exposed to his will. Propped on his elbows, hands locked behind my head, his mouth to my ear moaning how good I feel, he is rocking his stiff meat against the seam of my shorts, making me want him inside of me!

"Do you really want me to let you go?" His low baritone caresses my ear.

Sliding his erection up and down my crotch, I can feel his muscles all over my body.

"No, no I don't. I want you to fuck me. Fuck me just like this!"

"That's what I like to hear."

Releasing one of my arms, my skillful opponent maintains his lock on my other arm, pulls down my shorts and panties enough to expose my juicy fruit, and helps himself to me. Holding my left arm behind my head and grasping my right thigh, he drives into me with athletic proficiency. He works on me until we are both sweating and needing more! He fucks me deep and he rides me hard, then he grinds me slow before he pumps into me fast. Finally ready to release me, he lays on his back, pulls me onto him, and holds my hips down while he fucks my pussy until I dig into his massive chest and explode on his yummy piece! I work through the explosion, riding him like a bucking bull! He thrusts up, and I meet him, grinding down hard! He maintains his grasp on my hips, bangs deep into me and watches me caress my own tits while my muscles grips him, signaling another rapidly approaching eruption!

"I'm on my way baby! Ride this dick! Shit! Pop that pussy for me!"

I work on him until we are both drained. My candy sweet cream coats his gorgeous piece as I slow down and roll out the remaining juices from my delicious center.

Essence K. Berry

Every Lady is a Woman,
but Every Woman is NOT a Lady

A lesson in control, domination, and submission is best learned on the coat tails of multiple orgasms. Maybe I'll learn that lesson after round two!

Every Lady is a Woman,
but Every Woman is NOT a Lady

Lesson #2: "Ladies keep their dresses down!"

I say my goodbyes and switch my phone off so I can shower my 80 pound child of a canine with some well deserved attention. I must give her the expected quality time she knows and loves or she is not happy! Like clockwork, I prepare her for our regularly scheduled evening walk. After disconnecting my chat, I leave my home with remnants of the recent conversation on my mind...

Today he disclosed to me how enthralled he was when he initially laid eyes on me that warm spring day. He described the sway of my hips as I sauntered down the street; in no hurry at all, strolling and enjoying the sun kissing my skin. My gait was easy and my skirt was breezy. Never giving much thought to the effect my womanly curves had on men, I was taken aback when I observed this stranger's blatant stare. It was almost rude; gawking perhaps! When his eyes failed to meet mine even as I came to a standstill, I finally snapped at him, asking what exactly he was looking at. His quit wit, I would come to learn, resulted in an amazing recovery as he claimed to be distracted by the shine of my shoes! Likely story, I thought, but since that was the story he was selling, I decided to buy it. This stranger intrigued me and his mind worked in rapid succession, noticeably trying to concoct his next move. It helped that he had the markings of a hulk-like man.

Even as he engaged me in animated conversation that first day, I allowed myself to daydream about mounting his muscular thighs, grinding on his manhood, and feeling his strong hands all over my body. I could almost feel him behind me, thrusting viciously into me while he grasps my hair and holds my shoulders, forcing me to take every inch of his massive erection! His package is full and I yearn to be invaded by it, see how much of it I can take! I lose myself in my own erotic

Every Lady is a Woman, but Every Woman is NOT a Lady

fantasies when our paths cross. I remain the lady in the presence of the man who is attempting to court me. Our chance meetings eventually turn into frequent interactions. All the while, I try to tame the beast that claws and scratches to feed her hot desire each time he is near.

Today, he went through great lengths to tempt the beast out of me during one of those "coincidental" meetings in our small community. He ran into me, offering to walk with me for the duration of my outing, since I concluded our telephone conversation earlier. I can feel my wicked beast stir when he brushes his hand across the small of my back, but I quickly recover, determined to maintain my ladylike demeanor.

We reach his garage and in an effort to maintain my sweet disposition, I decline his offer to come into his place, using my pet as an excuse to remain in a relatively public setting. The garage door is open, the space is clean and empty, save one chair in the empty space. I accept his offer for water and watch as he tenderly waters my furry companion. His caring hand makes my lady parts moist and begs the attention of my wicked inner fiend. Deciding not to push against her so hard, I don't resist him when he pulls me into his lap for a short break. It is then that he reminds me this was the very same skirt I was wearing when he saw me the first day we spoke. Draping my arms around his neck, I allow him to position me over the growing mound in his lap. He attempts to raise my skirt, and I reflexively yank it back down!

"A lady would NEVER be caught with her skirt up!"

With a look of mischief dancing across his lips, he agrees it wouldn't be proper, especially if someone should come to visit and he had my skirt up around my waist. However, that didn't keep him from holding my

Every Lady is a Woman,
but Every Woman is NOT a Lady

waist and encouraging me back and forth on his erection until my panties were soaked with desire! Burying his warm mouth in the depths of my cleavage, I allow his hands to travel underneath my skirt's edge. I want his hands underneath my skirt, want his hands gripping my ass, and want these barriers from between us! I ache to have him deep inside of me! Stretching onto my tiptoes because my feet barely touch the ground, I encourage him to explore further, feeling the tug of his strong hands on my panties. To his credit, my skirt stays down!

With heavenly kneading motions, he managed to pull my panties down to my thighs, exposing my throbbing wetness to the material of his pants. Lust fills his eyes as he pushes my hips toward his knees.

"Stand up."

I follow his instruction, my hands on his shoulders, panties around my thighs. His eyes never leave mine as he runs his hands underneath my skirt and urges my panties down to my ankles.

"Your skirt is still down. Right?"

I nod recognition of his efforts and step out of my panties, watching as he takes them and places them in the pocket of his pants so they don't touch the ground.

"Babe, um, my dog can see us."

I am suddenly apprehensive about being observed so intently by my canine companion even though she is tethered to a post.

"It's natural and she isn't paying attention. Just sit back down like you were."

I watch as he releases his manhood from beneath his waistband. His piece springs up as if relieved to be out and my knees grow weak! Gathering my skirt, he draws me back to his lap, repositioning me so he can slide his pole into my wetness. I'm apprehensive now that I have seen him in his entirety, but I want him to fuck me so bad I quiver at his touch!

Acknowledging my gentle tremors, he takes pause, places his hands underneath my bottom, and gently spreads my cheeks. He places his fingers inside of me, clenching his jaw and watches my reaction as he slides his fingers deeper into me. Wanting more, I roll my hips, generating more moisture, more heat, relaxing and needing him now!

"Yeah, relax baby. Relax. You ready for me?" he whispers against my neck.

"Ummm hmmm, I am. I am."

Resuming my position on my tip toes, I take a deep breath, grip his massive joy stick in my hand, and slip down onto him. The head of his dick pierces my love and sends waves of pleasure and pain through my center! The intensity rocks my body! I want to withdraw from his entry into my body, but the pain is astounding, and my body begs for more!

I heave my hips down further, rolling them around, slamming them down with more force, striving to take him in deeper! He feels so good and all I want is to squirt my hot juices all over his thick pole! Keeping his promise, he keeps my skirt down, grips my back, and thrusts himself into me so deep it feels like I will explode from the pounding! I hold his shoulders while I grind on him, bursting out orgasm after orgasm!

"Fuck this pussy, baby! Yeah! Fuck me harder! Please! Harder!"

His chest ripples as he tightens his grip on my ass, slamming me down onto his thick rod, fucking me to a state of blinding delight! Humming at first until I escalate into a full blown scream, I take his meat until he growls and erupts into me with such a force he is

Every Lady is a Woman,
but Every Woman is NOT a Lady

reduced to shaking! All the while, my skirt never comes up! It is possible to be a lady and still feed the beast....

Essence K. Berry

Every Lady is a Woman,
but Every Woman is NOT a Lady

Lesson #3: *"A lady never bends over; she carefully stoops."*

Following the great garage escapade and the steamy ride on my lover's love stick, our encounters are more and more frequent and always gratifying. This particular day was spent in bed, lazily exploring one another. Rubbing, kissing, cuddling, and endless sexing. I have grown more comfortable with him laying me down, filling me with his thick muscle, as he knows how deep to go into me and doesn't just plunge mercilessly into my tightness. I am fine with him repositioning my legs from around his waist to the bend of his arms. It excites me when he rolls his hips slowly, winding into me with familiar strokes, then places my ankles around his neck while he braces on his knees and drives wildly into me while he speaks to me through clenched teeth, drizzling drops of sweat onto my naked nipples. The day goes on like this well into the afternoon.

Every Lady is a Woman,
but Every Woman is NOT a Lady

He pulls me to my feet following one of our cool down sessions. Guiding me until I am standing over him, my legs straddled either side of his damp body, he takes a moment to gaze up at me as I stand on his bed. He takes his swelling manhood in his hand and begins to stroke it while he takes in the view of my body over his. My body grows hot under his blazing gaze.

"Come straight down this time. Squat on this dick, don't ride me like a jockey this time."

"But I don't think my legs are long enough to do that."

"Trust me. I've got you."

Determined not to over think it, I plant my feet firmly by his hips and aim for the pole he holds in his hand. Offering his free hand for support, I take it and maneuver my sweet spot cautiously down onto the mushroom-like head of his arousal. Instinctively, my knees clamp together as his head pierces my opening, sending fire through my center!

"Easy; take your time."

He watches intently as I draw in a deep breath, apprehensive about allowing his mass further into me.

Sliding his big hands down my thighs for reassurance, he caresses them and urges my knees apart. I reposition myself, leaning further back, supporting myself on his thighs and rocking my hips forward. He gives back just enough to glide further into my constricted opening. I manage to allow him in past his thick head and the remaining entry is less invasive.

Sending tingles to the tip of my nipples and popping chills down my back, the force of his body entering mine is explosive and exciting! I press further, thrusting my hips, spreading my thighs more, wanting him deeper in me! The sensation is hot like white coals, stinging my inner walls, and consuming my lady part to the middle of my body! God help me, I want more!

His girth is almost painful and it pulls my swollen lips inward. I want more! I use my own small hand to spread my lips and plunge harder onto his fantastic erection. I continue to hold my lips open so he can watch me take his dick over and over again. Bouncing with repeated intentional thrusts up and down on his dick, I spread my thighs as far as they will stretch and lean back, holding my pussy lips for him, so he can enjoy the view as much as I enjoy the ride.

"Get ready baby. I'm about to cum on this dick and I want you to cum with me! Agh! You're too big! You feel so good! Fuck me harder! Harder baby! I'm cumin'"

Practically jumping up and down on his stiff meat, I release my lips and grasp both my breasts while he holds me steady at my hips and kills my pussy with equal drive into me! When the flood gates open, I roll around on his dick, relishing in the sensation of his dick on my pearl with each rotation!

Placing his thumb between my clit and his body, he massages my clit, drawing more sweet juices from my body until I think I will lose my mind! I soak his body, squirting my delicious nectar onto his lap, all over his hand, and waxing his glorious arousal! Finally, digging into my ass with both hands until he threatens to draw blood, my lover joins me in an awesome release that courses through me like a mighty flood. Just when I think the day is done, I shower, and prepare to return to my home....

Humming a satisfied tune after a glorious shower, I forget my training and bend right over in front of my lover to retrieve the clothes I deposited on the floor hours earlier. Naked, with a beautifully swollen pussy, I underestimate this man's stamina.

"Don't stand up. Stay there; just like that!"

Every Lady is a Woman,
but Every Woman is NOT a Lady

I dare to take a glimpse behind me, wondering what the problem is and I am greeted by my lover's generous erection. Excited, I do as I am told and hold my position. I barely have time to lock the lady away as she admonishes me for bending over in such a scandalous manner before I release the beast who is yelling for more, more, MORE!

With no foreplay at all, he greedily attacks my cheeks, spreading them to fully expose my damp pus, and plunges into me, moaning about the delicious view I presented him when I bent over! I take the spanking, wanting more, throwing my ass back to him. I wiggle my hips, part my thighs, and beg him to fuck me harder! Holding the front of my thighs, he pulls me to him and drives so deep I can feel his sack meeting my wetness with each blow! Hitting me quickly with hard strokes until he emanates a continuous high pitched tone, he rides my ass until I am quivering! Relentless, he takes

Every Lady is a Woman,
but Every Woman is NOT a Lady

me down to the bed, and continues the pace until he can only hold my shoulders and pump in and out of me until he is drained of the intensity that brought us here. He slows his pace, digging deep into me while I lay prostate on his bed and we grind until we have both satisfied our carnal desires. Damn, if that's what I get when I bend over in front of a man, I'll take it!

Every Lady is a Woman,
but Every Woman is NOT a Lady

Lesson #4: *"A Lady does not sweat; she glistens"*

The lady in me tries not to let him see me sweat; however, the athlete in me loves physical interaction! I live for the taut muscles, the thrill of the ride, and the exhilaration of the physical release that accompanies the orgasm! I love it all! My lover is a sexual athlete and he caters to my needs until I have had enough.

I attempt to present the lady I have been raised to be in public. Subsequently, I keep finding myself in situations with my untamed beast taking over. I welcome the opportunity to be myself without reservation with my lover. This man allows me to have my way with him each time we are together. Naked in his bed with just the sound of the rotation of the ceiling fan above, my mind is clear and my beast is free to roam...

Long after our clothes have been shed and we have petted, stroked and teased one another to arousal, he relinquishes control of our lovemaking. He feels great beneath me; warm, solid, and filling my lady parts up! There is only one thing on my mind- I want to fuck him long and hard until my muscles scream! I have to take him from the top so I can control the depth of penetration, as his piece is a lot to take. As many times as we have been together, I still have to take a deep breath before allowing his entrance into my body!

I relax my love muscle, hold on to his erection, and prepare for the introduction into my sweet spot. Ascending slowly onto his thick pole, I take him in, a little at a time, then deep into my love, and work on his willing muscle until my thighs burn and a thin trickle of sweat streams down the middle of my back.

"You feel so good! I could ride this dick all day..."

I continue rolling my ass on his lengthy piece, saturating his thighs with the moisture from my body. I place my hands flat on the hairy surface of his massive chest for leverage. Everything about my lover speaks male! His scent, the soft hair that covers his hard body, the full lips that shape his large mouth! While I bounce on his thick erection, I watch his massive hands palm my full breasts and guide them to his voluptuous mouth. His tongue seeks my body, lapping my nipples like sweet candy, calling them to attention. I grind and he sucks.

I palm his big bald head and encourage him further. I need more! "Suck them harder baby. That feels *so* good! Suck them hard!"

He reciprocates, mouth gaping, taking my nipples then my full breasts deep into his mouth. He nibbles, then bites them gently, before sucking them harder. My body responds to the piercing pain he inflicts on my voluptuous breasts as I ride him harder! I tuck my feet underneath his strong legs and slam down harder on his stiff erection!

*Every Lady is a Woman,
but Every Woman is NOT a Lady*

"Just like that baby! Give me this dick! Fuck this pussy!"

Rolling my nipples between his teeth, pulling my tender flesh further into his inviting mouth until I scream, he thrusts his hips harder into my grinding pelvis, matching my rhythm and my powerful thrusts. My face is wet with lustful perspiration. The ladies would be mortified, as I am way beyond the point of glistening! I ride him until I am drenched! My neck, my shoulders, my arms, and my chest shimmer with a thin coat of moisture. My body on his body, creates a simmering friction that makes a sex induced cocktail! I embrace him fully, my nipples against his solid chest. He encourages my thighs further apart, grasping my hips as he delivers his muscle deeper into me. My body is soaked and my muscles are taut, yet my lustful beast screams for more!

Every Lady is a Woman,
but Every Woman is NOT a Lady

Up and down I glide, caressing his body while I grind my hips against his hips; pulling him further into me, filling my Pretty Girl with his thickness until we are both drenched in our desires. He closes his eyes and tightens his handle on my ass while I drain him. He suckles my breasts while my love muscle milks him of the final drops of his delicious cream. I slowly roll my sweet ass on his lap while he helps himself to my perky nipples until we are both spent. My beast is a very satisfied, "glistening" young lady! Breaking that rule was well worth it!

Every Lady is a Woman,
but Every Woman is NOT a Lady

Lesson #5: "*A lady is NEVER to drink from a bottle!*"

Tonight is supposed to be the party of the year. I wonder how it will differ from last week's party of the year and the party of the year the week before that I one. My roommate swears this week's affairs will bring a new vibe to our scene. There has been heavy promotion all over the campus about the infamous Yak Boyz bringing their electric party style to town and it has the whole campus buzzing! The Yak Boyz are rapidly gaining acclaim at college campuses all over and their next stop is to our university! I've heard these guys bring a wild party with their Cognac infused vibe, leaving a white hot trail for others to try to follow. Of course an entire crew of promoters, DJ's, and producers bound over an appreciation of a good Cognac, mixed with the business sense to orchestrate a raw party, is the epitome of my kind of scene. My roomy left me to go on what

Essence K. Berry

Every Lady is a Woman, but Every Woman is NOT a Lady

has become our traditional pre-party beer run, so I take advantage of the alone time to start my groove early.

The evening is warm and the excitement in the air is electric. The music pours through the room, enticing my hips to move to and fro. I let the rhythm send me into a relaxing trance. The thumping coordinates with my pulse, taking me to a world filled with brilliant colors, cool breezes, and sensational aromas. I love the transformation of music! It speaks to every one of my senses and I tend to get lost in it. I close my eyes and allow my body to ride the deep waves that penetrate throughout the room.

Suddenly my musical serenity is disrupted by the delivery of our spirits for the night! Bottles are being placed down and bags are being rattled. My friend has finally returned with our libation, but is escorted by two gentleman guests. Overlooking the disturbance, I continue my slow wind as my roommate makes introductions between myself and the stranger who joins us. My body hums with a twinge of euphoria. I recognize my friend's companion, but his yummy friend is unfamiliar. I open my dance area in response, welcoming him into my embrace. He gladly joins me, wrapping me in his arms, and falls into step with me as if we have danced to this groove a million times before. I welcome his warm hands over my curves as he sways with me. I get a close look at him and smile before closing my eyes again. I am free to let my mind wonder, concentrating on his soft tenor in my ear, complimenting my scent and my womanly physique. Kissing me behind my ear, holding me from behind, he tells me he would be willing to bet I taste as tantalizing as I smell. At that point, the sensuous beast in me dances right up to the surface and takes control of the slow two step we are engaged in.

Every Lady is a Woman,
but Every Woman is NOT a Lady

My eyes spring open, yanking me from my sea of tranquility, and my wheels start turning! My mischievous little monster was already scratching at the surface, anxious to make an appearance, but my partner's little "bet" has opened the flood gates! She is free, excited, and ready to dive right into whatever he has in mind. There is nothing like a good old fashioned wager to excite my little monster! With a simple twirl, I am face to face with my dance partner. He has a delicious mouth, naughty eyes, and a very masculine body. My curiosity is piqued!

"What do you have in mind?"

He appears startled by my forward nature, but takes it in stride, attempting to maintain his laid back demeanor. I like it when a man is up for a little adventure! My little beast is all giddy! Kissing me softly on my face, then on my neck, my companion knows he has my attention.

Every Lady is a Woman,
but Every Woman is NOT a Lady

"Are you serious? You would let me smell you?" He inhales deeply at the base of my neck... "Taste you?" Whisper soft kisses linger along my collar bone... "Lick you?" His warm tongue caresses the side of my mouth as he locks his eyes on mine.

"You bet I would. You did say bet, right? What exactly are we betting?"

We are interrupted by an almost frantic outcry, "Please don't bet with her! She can't walk away from a bet and you will never win! She refuses to lose! Come on, let's go to the party!"

This seems to add fuel to the fire, as my dance partner lights up! "Oh! In that case, I'm taking this one! *Anything* I say?" He virtually coos into my ear as we continue the remnants of our slow grind.

"Absolutely! You're a big boy! I believe you will pay up when you lose." We maintain eye contact and I can see the twinkle in his eye as he conjures up the bet...

"My buddy and I just purchased beer. I choose the bottle. If you can finish your bottle before I finish mine, I get to smell you-all over; then taste you and lick you until you *beg* me to stop! Agreed?"

My friend is desperately begging me to decline, but I absolutely can NOT! His friend is laughing a knowing laugh, because he has been out with us before and knows I can take him.

Ignoring my friend, I reach for my dance buddy's hand, give it a firm shake, and tell him he has a deal.

My challenger produces two of the most unbelievably large bottles of beer I have ever seen! Sixty four ounce bottles! This cannot be right! I am a little apprehensive, but a bet is a bet, so I am determined to give it the old college try! My friend whispers in my ear, "You know you don't have to do this, right?"

Every Lady is a Woman, but Every Woman is NOT a Lady

I follow my dance partner's hungry gaze as he allows his bold eyes to appraise my curves.

"Girl, did you see his lips? Ok, maybe you saw them, but you did not *feel* them! I intend to feel them all over my body! So don't get too comfy. Be prepared to take your drinks to go! Watch my cue and get out when I say!"

I take the bottle offered to me and the lady in me makes an appearance long enough to pass the bottle right back to him, affording him the gentleman's duty of removing the top for me. He chuckles, "Would the lady like a glass as well?"

I cast him a wicked glare before assuring him the lady can take it straight from the bottle. Taking a moment to run my tongue around the bottle's edge, and dip my lips around the opening down to the neck to prep my gag reflex, I give my friend the okay to start us off. I meet my competitor's hypnotic stare at the oral display

I've just performed on the bottle and inform him, "You didn't say what you get if I lose. No worries, you should just be ready to pay up. No need for a counter bet." With a confident wink, I am ready to begin.

Twinkle Toes is out of the starting gate, swallowing mouths full of the gold liquid down in massive gulps, stopping to breathe between swallows. My method differs drastically. I take steady pulls in, down my throat, while taking breaths in through my nose. I swallow, breathe, swallow, breathe…The pattern is effective and my mouth never fills up with the frothy brew like my challenger's does. I keep my eyes on him as I continue my steady ascension to the bottom of the massive vessel. He isn't half way through his attempt at emptying his bottle; filling his mouth, gulping it down, then fighting for air before plunging in again! The technique is grossly laborious, ineffective, and I find it quite humorous! He's cute and determined!

Every Lady is a Woman,
but Every Woman is NOT a Lady

My adversary's friend lets out a long whistle…"Man, are you really going to let this five foot nothing girl outdrink you?! You are sooo weak!" His laughter pierces the music pulsing through the room.

I'm more than three quarters of the way through my bottle now and he still struggles to reach his halfway point. I continue my swallow-breathe method and use my right foot to push off my left boot. My friend takes this as her cue and grabs her companion. "They'll meet us at the party Baby. We should be out of here before she finishes. Anyway, it looks like it's time for your friend to pay up!"

I manage to maintain my footing as the effect of the malted liquid begins to swirl about my head. Unbuttoning my jeans while I drag the swallows of the cold liquid down my throat, I nod toward the door, acknowledging it is okay for the other couple to make their way out.

Essence K. Berry

Every Lady is a Woman,
but Every Woman is NOT a Lady

"Unbelievable man! Un-fucking-believable! I'll grab your man card later at the party! She had better show up smiling too! Congrats little lady! Have fun! Shit! You deserve it!"

With an air of confidence, my friend whispers to my companion, "I told you she doesn't like to lose." With that utterance, we were left alone as the door closed behind them.

Wordlessly, my opponent accepts his defeat and comes closer to pay his debt to me. "Are you really okay? That was a lot to take down."

He kisses my chin…

"So much for a little lady."

He removes the now empty bottle from my hand and kisses my palm with his seductive lips…

"A bet is a bet, right?"

His mouth caresses the base of my throat.

"Lay down little lady."

Every Lady is a Woman, but Every Woman is NOT a Lady

I follow his instruction and recline onto the bed. He relieves me of my other boot, finishes removing my jeans and takes special care with my panties. I am lightheaded and giggling victoriously, but I tingle from anticipation. As promised, my partner takes his time parting my thighs, inhaling my warm scent, and burying his nose between my lips. His breath is warm and his mouth is a pleasure source. He kisses my hot spot, breathes me in, and methodically licks me until the roll of my hips answer the call of his tongue. I am clearly riding a cloud of drunken ecstasy as he licks, sucks, and devours my sweet delectable. Twinkle Toes satisfies me on my back, spreading my thighs, and slurping my nectar until I squeal. I rub his head, pinch my nipples, and explore my own wetness created by the darting and lapping of his skillful tongue. I watch him kiss my swollen lips, tease me pearl, and plunge his tongue into my juicy opening with long, steady strokes. He tickles me softly, he nibbles me, and he wraps his arms around my thighs and sucks me until I scream! He rolls me onto my stomach, before pulling me to my knees, and sucks my Pretty Girl from behind until I fear I will pass out in my buzzed haze! My dance partner delivers everything he dared to promise. He is tactical, exquisite, and an oral artist of sorts.

When I finally fear I cannot possibly release one more expulsion from my body, he pulls me into a sitting position, asking me if he has fulfilled his end of the bet. Focusing on his handsome features through a tipsy fog, I hold his face in my hands and kiss his exquisitely shaped mouth, taking in the sweet cocktail he has created between my thighs on his lips.

"Paid in full Baby."

"Good. And for the record, you do taste as good as you smell."

Every Lady is a Woman,
but Every Woman is NOT a Lady

We get ourselves together so we can rejoin the other couple. As promised, I arrive with a smile on my face!

Thanks to my dance partner, I don't think I will ever drink from a glass again!

Every Lady is a Woman,
but Every Woman is NOT a Lady

Lesson #6: "A lady sits with her legs closed"

As I sit on the front porch one scorching summer night with my male suitor, reveling in the occasional whisper of air that graces us periodically, the stars are shining, my clothes are sticking to me, and he can't keep his eyes off of my thighs. The heat between us is simmering hotter than what permeates the night air. I follow all of the rules of entertaining a gentleman: I make sure he arrives to visit me at a descent hour; I keep the level of conversation at a respectable tone; and I make sure to offer him a cold beverage when he arrives. I am the epitome of the well trained young lady.

My suitor's visits tend to ride on the tails of the setting sun, as the squelching daytime heat is enough to render a fainting spell in the strongest of men. I watched his shoulders sway as he approached me, calling forth additional heat between my thighs. His powerful thighs, small waist, and broad shoulders sing to my body, beckoning my naughty side to the surface. *Be good! Keep cool! Be mindful of your actions young lady!* I try to stifle my tawdry side, but he makes my body hot without ever touching me! So few men have that effect on me. This man's very presence is enough to awaken my senses and shift my desires into overdrive. When we get together, the yearning is virtually tangible!

This evening he makes no attempt to mask his obvious approval as he comes closer to where I am sitting. I love that he is unapologetic as his eyes take my body in. Rethinking my positioning in front of the porch, I decide to test his adventuresome side. I try to be the lady and conduct myself accordingly, but it is increasingly difficult with every step he takes closer to me. *Take deep breaths and exercise some self-control! This is neither the time nor the place!*

I continue to converse with my gentleman caller, but I am not blind. Following his gaze as it travels along

Every Lady is a Woman,
but Every Woman is NOT a Lady

the length of my legs; I intentionally scoot to the edge of the porch and place my right foot flat on the top step, enjoying the welcome relief of a slight breeze all the way up the crotch of my shorts. Observing his not so conspicuous gaze to the area the breeze traveled to, I rub my inner thigh for emphasis. I can no longer contain the monstrous urges screaming to escape!

"See something you like?"

Adjusting the instant erection that speaks volumes before he has a chance to form audible words, he steps closer and states the obvious to me.

"You do know when you cock your leg up that high I can see your lips and cheeks, don't you?"

Leaning back and placing my hands flat on the porch behind me, I roll my hips slowly forward, affording him a good look.

"Is that a fact? Think that's why my Mama always told me to keep my knees together and cross my legs when I sit? Maybe you should come closer so the passersby don't get a peek at my goodies."

Daring to take another apprehensive step closer, my companion is near enough that I can feel the heat from his muscular body.

"Closer," I invite him quietly. "Kiss me."

Careful to observe our surroundings first, he places his hands softly on my thighs and leans in to place a feather light kiss to my lips. I can taste the faint trace of the cigarette he smoked on the short walk to my place. The mixture of his vice and his manly scent in the summer evening is tantalizing to me as I lean in to breathe his intoxicating aroma in. I become increasingly aware of his reservation about displaying too much public affection, especially in his current state of arousal. However, I am feeling especially daring and my naughty little beast is clawing away, anxious to come out and play!

Every Lady is a Woman, but Every Woman is NOT a Lady

I wrap my other leg around his gorgeous bowed leg and pull him closer to my womanly warmth. He allows his hands to venture up my thighs, along the curve of my hips, and cup my soft backside, bringing me right to the edge of my sitting place. I literally have to hold on to him to keep my balance, as I am perched on the edge of the porch with my leg still high on the step beside me.

He kisses me deeper, lost in the feel of his body against mine. My lover grips my ass with firm hands while he pulls my tongue into his mouth. Relaxing into his embrace, wanting more of him, I roll my tongue around his, stroking the top of the sweet flesh with mine. I open my mouth for him, spread my thighs further for him, and welcome him to feel me further.

"Ummm, you smell so good," comes his heavy baritone as he kisses my neck. I allow my head to roll back welcoming further exploration.

Every Lady is a Woman,
but Every Woman is NOT a Lady

"So do you. I want you *so* bad!"

"Right now?"

"Yeah baby! See!" I place his hand between my thighs, so he can feel the moisture his presence is generating.

Eagerly following my lead, he caresses my exposed lips with his fingers, as my panties do not quite cover the thickness of my lips. Slipping his fingers into the side of my panties, he releases a low moan.

"Ooo girl! This fat pussy is gonna get us both in trouble! We can't do this out here!"

Yet he continues to finger my Pretty Girl with hands of a man who is no stranger to hard work. His fingers trace my thick lips, dip in and out of my wetness, and strum the growing pearl that begs for more! He has reservations, yet he fucks me with his hand until I am crawling against the hardness of his ample manhood! The lady in me loses out as my animal practically begs him to take me!

I open my thighs even more for him, rub my Pretty Girl against his crotch, and lick his neck, drawing him into me with my legs.

"Fuck me baby. Right now." I pull the front of his shorts down and stroke him.

"We can't do this here. People are driving down the street. Damn you are so wet! The neighbors may be looking! Hell, the sun just barely went down!"

I kiss him to quiet his chatter while I rub my own wet pussy then stroke his meat. His knees seem to buckle a little when the juices from my love moisten his piece, so I tighten my grip around his leg with mine.

Sliding my panties further to the side, I slide his head up and down my moist crevice, from my hot pearl to my wet opening.

"Just come straight into me slowly Baby. Just like that. Anyone passing by will just think you are hugging me. Ooo yeah. Just like that. "

I guide his thick pole into my wetness and take a deep breath as I glide him deeper into me.

"Ummm hmmm, don't pump or thrust too much. Oh yeah. Just keep pushing. Slowly. Oh yeah Baby. Yeah! Just like that!" My mouth to his ear delivering low coaxing instruction, he continues to delve deeper into me, slowly, purposefully.

"I must...SHIT! Be crazy. Shit you feel good. We can't do this out here. Ooo you feel good!" His descent into my throbbing pussy continues as does his moral struggle.

I wrap my arms tightly around his neck and he engulfs me in an embrace that threatens to crack my ribs. With barely visual thrusts, my suitor delivers himself slowly into me so deep he feels like he is in the depths of my stomach. He holds me at the edge of the porch, in that unladylike position with my leg up, while

Every Lady is a Woman,
but Every Woman is NOT a Lady

I gently begin to bounce up and down on his stiffness, grinding out orgasms that rock my body and make his strong legs tremor! I grip his meat with my muscles, squeezing my ass as I pull up to the tip of his meat, then slide back down while he drives deep back into me. His motions are steady, penetrating deep, allowing me to rock up and down on the edge of my perching spot. He holds me with strong hands, giving me what I need until I am done. When I have adequately satisfied the beast in me and properly drained my companion of his powerful load, he pulls his capable hands from beneath my ass and requests that I only wear these shorts behind closed doors with him, because there is NOTHING ladylike about them....

*Every Lady is a Woman,
but Every Woman is NOT a Lady*

Lesson #7 "A lady is groomed at all times"

Our little front porch courtship evolves into us moving in together further down the road. He quickly learns my grooming habits and looks forward to a few of them, knowing I perform them nightly. As much as I have tried to uphold this lesson in life, my sweetie would not allow me to be a proper lady! Fresh out of the shower, performing my ritualistic grooming, he rounds the corner to find me bent over deep at the waist, brushing my hair upside down to add the expected volume, as I was always taught to do. After all, a woman's hair is her crowning glory and I have a healthy mane of it! It takes time and attention to keep it beautiful. Obviously he has been there for a moment observing, as he has grown a healthy erection from the view. My companion approaches me from behind, letting me feel his growing appreciation, pressing it firmly between the cheeks of my barely covered ass, enticing the sensitive space between my thighs. Pretending to ignore him, I continue brushing my hair and remain unresponsive as my Pretty Girl starts to throb with anticipation. He likes attention and when I refuse to acknowledge him, he usually makes every effort to leave a lasting impression to teach me a lesson about ignoring him. It's a sadistic game we play! Tonight, I shall bring him to a boiling point!

Reaching forward, he runs his hands thru my hair as I continue to brush it, gripping firmly from the roots before tugging my head upward toward the mirror. Our eyes meet seconds before he takes the crotch of my high cut panties and pulls them tightly into my ass. He wants me to witness him take possession of my body as much as my little beast desires to watch! Knowing I like the sensation of the tension of the material against my tiny pearl and the pull between my thick lips, he holds my gaze as I arch into his begging meat. He practically dares me to respond to him with the glint in his eyes! That simple look between us locks the lady in me down and sets my giddy beast bursting from within! He is about to fuck me hard and my beast is excited and geared up for the ride!

"Are you just going to bone me, or are you going to get in my pussy?"

Without unlocking my gaze from his, I reach back to remove my panties, but his grip on my hair hinders my full range of motion. Noting my struggle, he is elated by the power he has over me. My lover is considerable taller than I am, but is determined to control the situation. Tugging tighter on my locks, he dips down and pushes up, driving his pelvis further into my throbbing muffin until the front of my thighs are flush against the vanity area. Grinding his meat against my swelling pussy until I am pleading with my eyes for him to fuck me right now, he pulls my head back and bites me on the side of my neck. I want him in me! I can almost feel him penetrating me, but I am too stubborn to beg for it! Besides, he is enjoying the control! Smug son of a bitch!

I watch his eyes as he intentionally works his well-muscled body against mine as if he is already fucking me. He pulls my hair hard, runs his hands underneath my shirt and has his way with my full tits. I refuse to let him break me! Spreading my thighs further apart, I submit to his calculated thrusts and even join in his rhythmic motion, giving it right back to him. Maintaining eye contact, I slip my hand into the front of my panties, manipulating my throbbing clit, bringing myself to a sweet orgasm!

"Get in me now. Right now! Cum with me Baby! Ohhh yeah, cum with me!"

"Damn right! And you will cum for me again!"

Every Lady is a Woman,
but Every Woman is NOT a Lady

Exposing my pussy, taking his time to squeeze it, grip it, and move his fingers into me so he can feel my wetness, he curses me underneath his breath for my self-induced orgasm. The girth of his fingers is mesmerizing! Pulling his fingers slowly out and sliding his throbbing arousal into my already pulsating pus, I watch him thrust into me in the mirror. Slowly at first, he pushes into me, feeling the squeeze of my already contracting muscles as he dives deeper. Oh how I waited the entry! He fits like a glove! Thick, hard, and deep into me, making me watch, as he keeps my head pulled upward! Each thrust into me equates a tug on my hair! It's all control for him and I love it!

Holding my hair with one hand and bracing on the small of my back with the other, he strokes me deep, delivering powerful thrusts while we eye one another in the mirror. I can see my breasts jiggle with each blow to my backside. The satisfaction that clouds my pretty

Every Lady is a Woman, but Every Woman is NOT a Lady

features are second only to the beauty of the motion of his hips grinding into me! I watch his face draw tight and he fucks me harder and faster, dancing deeper into my body as I receive him with gleeful thrusts. The pussy is good to him. Oh yeah, it's good. He is in full plow mode and it's all over his face! He is fucking me wild and hard now and trying to maintain control. His face and his grip on my hair scream his pleasure to me! He is about to cum soon and I want to cum with him!

"Is that dick good Baby? Is it good? Fuck it! Take all of it! Take that dick! Bounce that ass on it!"

I take the raw beating of his meat into my Pretty Girl. I take it deep; I take it slow and I take it long! Finally I take it fast and hard until I explode with him! He's not done with me yet. He rocks my thighs into the vanity once more, pulling my knee onto the surface, then pounds into me some more, forcing me to brace onto the mirror for support! Legs shaking and heart pounding

Every Lady is a Woman,
but Every Woman is NOT a Lady

with ecstasy, I meet his gaze one more time in the mirror when he releases his hold on my hair and wraps his arms underneath mine, gripping my tits as he empties into me again! I brace on the vanity and grind out the last of my steamy juices onto his monstrous muscle.

Breathless, I meet his satisfied gaze in the mirror, touch my hair as I examine it, and inform him with a gratified smile, "Damn, now I have to start all over." A lady's grooming is never done....

Every Lady is a Woman,
but Every Woman is NOT a Lady

Lesson #8: "A lady does not play with her food!"

What I love about my sweetie is our outings are as spontaneous and pleasurable as our intimate times together. Sure, we have hair pulling and wars of will at home, but our entertainment extends beyond that. I have enjoyed the concept of a picnic lunch for as far back as I can remember. It could be the sun's rays warming my skin; breathing in the fresh, crisp air; or the simple joy of dining outside. Whatever it is, I was thrilled when my companion recommended it!

Nothing says weekend picnic like crispy fried chicken, big juicy dill pickles, homemade potato salad made just right, sweet iced tea with a perfect hint of lemon, and summer sweetened watermelon! This beautiful creature of mine thought of everything! As our picnic is more reminiscent of supper, we bask in the quietening park as the families dispense for the evening. My sweetie hand feeds me from his plate, encouraging me to broaden my pallet. I am not as accustomed to the spicy delicacies as he is, and I am therefore reluctant to explore the juicy jalapeno pepper he offers me with the chicken from his plate. Determined, he holds my gaze as he squeezes the pepper onto the tip of his tongue and invites me to partake.

"Weren't you taught it's not nice to play with your food?" I return his sultry gaze and wait patiently for inevitable water works to begin, but it never does. He takes the scorching heat like a champion.

"Who's playing? Kiss me." He closes his mouth as if to seal in the searing flavor before leaning closer to me. The invitation is deliciously tempting, as his kisses are always delectable. Nevertheless, I remain apprehensive about the heat, the inevitable burn.

Unconsciously, my fingers navigate to my lips and I inquire honesty about the heat. With a slow exaggeration, he swipes his tongue across his lips and assures me it is all good. Straddling the park bench facing him, I release my guard, lean in to him, and allow his moistened lips to caress mine. The tingle is gradual; creeping almost! Reflexively, I pull away and put my fingers to my lips again, as if this would soothe the fire.

Delighted by my reaction, he soothes my lips further with a cube of ice from his glass.

"Better Baby?"

I can only stare at him, startled by the burning sensation, yet curiously aroused! As if reading my mind, he releases his tongue from his gorgeous mouth again and drips juice from the fiery morsel. Pulling me from behind my knees, he closes the space between our bodies, draping my thighs so they fall over his, allowing my feet to dangle freely. My crotch rests directly in front of his, allowing him to wrap his arms around my waist and pull me in for the most heated kiss I have ever experienced! His lips consume mine, his tongue dances with mine, and his scorching fingertips sear each part of my body they come in contact with!

His masculine fingers journey down the back of my shorts, gripping my bare skin, pulling me even closer to his growing erection. My body responds to his, arching against him, practically running from the blistering intrusion, yet wanting more!

His hands travel up my back, searching for the hooks he is sure secures the garment that hold my buxom breasts securely in place. His escapades leave streaks of heat on my moist skin, which sends warm sensations all over me! The flames licking my back threaten to overtake me as his kisses travel over my face and down the hollow of my neck! The evening air stings my lips and assault me in each place he trails his blazing, wet mouth. The sensation is alarming, still I yearn for more!

Every Lady is a Woman,
but Every Woman is NOT a Lady

I feel the sizzle when his hands seek my plump breasts through the sheer lace of my bra's front. Following his hungry gaze to the swell of my breasts, I can no longer restrain the daring little fiend struggling to come out and play! Ignoring my upbringing and succumbing to my own curiosity, I take his spicy vegetation and dare to drizzle the juice down my voluptuous mounds, watching the trail run to my nipples and drip from the lacy material. I look up to meet his gaze, just as he lowers his head to follow suit! Kissing my left nipple through the lace, then my right, I am impressed by his diligence, his attentiveness, the care he takes breathing in the spicy scent of the juice on my body. Palming my back and thrusting my chest into his mouth, he bites my neck, sucking it until it singes me, before licking the remaining liquor from the stream I blazed down my body. The heat is searing through me, increasing my need for him!

Essence K. Berry

Every Lady is a Woman, but Every Woman is NOT a Lady

Face to face, his manhood stroking my warm feminine place through my shorts, I release the single hook from the front of my bra, welcoming his searing assault full onto my breasts! Each lick, each suck, every nibble and pull into his hot mouth sets another fire of desire in me! My beast has officially been poked and stirred!

My companion helps himself to every part of my body I expose to him! Still, I desires more! MORE!

Scooting back from his lap, I carefully survey the park, noting our only remaining companion is the twinge of light from the moon which seemingly dances on the lake before us.

As my lover commences to kneading my body with strong hands, I gladly submit to his exploration down the front of my shorts.

Essence K. Berry

*Every Lady is a Woman,
but Every Woman is NOT a Lady*

"So hot Babe! Agh! It's hot!" The initial contact with my moist flesh is breathtaking! I can barely breathe the words out!

"Would you like me to stop?"

In answer, I remove his hands from between my thighs, squeeze the molten liquid onto his fingertips, and slowly unzip my shorts. My companion urges me upward to the edge of the picnic table. Following my suggestive lead, he licks his fingertips before he pulls my shorts from underneath me. My lover positions himself in front of me as if anxiously awaiting a meal. I part my thighs slowly for him, with growing anticipation. Perched on the table, I nervously brace for his blazing mouth, his tongue of flames, his sizzling fingers, and his sweltering thumb to my throbbing centerpiece!

His soft lips to my wet center are flames, heating my body from the inside out! The warmth is so intense it

Essence K. Berry

is almost chilling! Yet, I can't get enough! I need it! I want it! Give me more!

"Shit! It's hot Baby! Ouch! It's hot!" I push his head away, then pull him in again! Legs trembling, the heat even penetrates when his mouth is away! "Don't stop! Ok wait! Now! Baby it burns! Suck me some more!" I'm conflicted between torturous pleasures!

His moist tongue probes my juicy folds, blazes flaming rings around my engorged clit, and finally he sucks hot fluid from my swollen love with lips kissed by intense flames! He holds my knees steady, as I resort to bucking for him, perched on the table's edge with my legs spread eagle on either side of his broad shoulders. The sensation is astounding, drawing tears of pleasure and pain from me involuntarily! I hold my companion's head, push it deeper into my pounding pus, and welcome his searing invasion into my eager body. Just as I feel the sweat trickle down the middle of my back and I cannot take another second of the heat coursing through me, my companion grips my thighs and pulls me in for more! He increases the suction on my clit as I ride the explosive waves over and over again! My lover alternates between lapping my fiery nectar with a full tongue, caressing my pearl with his pepper soaked thumbs until I pop my pussy for him, then blowing on the flames he creates until I shudder from hot chills!

I take the tongue lashing until my body is wet from the intensity of the heat. When I am reduced to moaning and my hips simply roll on the table to meet the rhythm of his strokes as he pulls the next orgasm from my depths, I can't imagine how his finale can possibly compare!

It's like a dream! I watch him part my thighs and place my feet on the bench beside him. "Are you okay Baby?"

Every Lady is a Woman,
but Every Woman is NOT a Lady

I simply nod as I reach down to stroke my Pretty Girl. He has left me practically purring after the oral assault he put on me. The trembling of my thighs has finally subsided, so I take a moment to lean back, close my eyes, and enjoy the whispering breeze.

My lover stands, his manhood pressing between my swollen lips through the material of his pants, as he pulls my nipples into his mouth and grinds against my opening.

Lazily, I open my eyes, drunk on his love, "Why don't you take that out and get in me?"

Never having to be told twice, my sweetie unleashes his astounding erection, drenches his hand in the juice from a fat jalapeno pepper, slides his palm up my wet pussy, and pushes himself into me!

"AGGGHHH! SHIT!" I bolt upright immediately and he is already holding firmly to me!

Every Lady is a Woman,
but Every Woman is NOT a Lady

"No Baby, no! Keep that sweet ass right there!" His lips move across my lips, encouraging, teeth gritting, admonishing me to hold my place..."Hold whatcha got baby...Oh yeah! Damn that IS hot! SHIT!" He thrusts harder, deeper into me, squeezing my ass and fucking me to a steady rhythm. "Ooo yeah, gimme that pussy!" His lips venture to my tits as they bounce with each forward thrust. "Ummm hmmm..." He hums as he delivers his pole of fire deeper into me... "Ride this dick Baby, RIDE IT!"

Like a puppet on a string, slave to his words, helpless to his erotic power, I grind my sweet pussy down on his dick with each up stroke into me. I roll my hips on the flaming rod he delivers into me; I grind harder as he fucks me harder; I place my hands flat on the table behind me for support and bounce my dripping mound on his thick erection while he pounds the bottom out of my pussy!

Essence K. Berry

"Look at those titties bounce!" He devours them with his hot mouth, driving me to a heat induced frenzy!

"Work that ass on this dick Baby, fuck it good!" I squirt hot juices down his piece, and he commands me further!

"Hold on to me Baby! Hold me!" He is standing in front of me in the same place he was sitting on the bench when he was licking me into oblivion. He takes his seat, pulling me into his lap in a squatting position over him. I hold onto his shoulders for support as he assures me he won't let go.

"Now go to work." I ride his flaming dick, legs wide open for him, up and down, hard, hot, and all the way into me until I cum so hard from the mixture of the pleasure and pain piercing through me, my vision is clouded with red and blue dots! All manners of sparkling colors burst in my mind's eye! The goosh of fluid finally subsides as I slow to a steady gyration in his

Every Lady is a Woman,
but Every Woman is NOT a Lady

lap, holding him chest to chest, massaging the remnants of my orgasm out as I roll my clit around on his softening shaft. I take a deep, satisfied breath as I know my naughty little beast is satisfied with her unladylike behavior. Content once again, I wonder if cold food is as exciting as the forbidden hot stuff!

Every Lady is a Woman,
but Every Woman is NOT a Lady

Lesson #9: "Ladies do not lick their fingers"

Everything about this man is tantalizing. The mixture of his masculine scent and musky cologne; the hungry look in his eye; the need in his touch when our bodies connect. It is difficult to maintain trying to get through a night out with him sometimes! The physical attraction to him is as strong as the attraction to his sweet personality. I desire every part of him. I want to feel, touch, taste, and explore every inch of him. My needs are definitely not those of a "nice" young lady. Therefore, I relieve the lady of her duties as soon as we are back from an evening out and unleash my temptress to come out and play!

Our encounters are sporadic, but always eventful. We settle in on a cool winter night with two glasses, a bottle of wine, and the low glow from the fireplace. I relax and allow the spirited libation to warm me throughout. The heat travels down my throat, entices my senses, and warms me all over. I close my eyes, the sensation continues to my limbs, and finally reaches the moist place that calls to me. When I open my eyes and lock in on my companion, my desires are mirrored in his gaze. We snuggle closer, exchange soft kisses, and the heat swelters between us.

I crave him from his thick wavy hair to his perfect toes. I carefully remove his glasses as he submits to my exploration. The fire whispers behind us. I lick his fingers, lazily tasting them individually. He extends each one, watching as I start at the tips with slow kisses, then suck them into my mouth, catering to each finger separately. He opens his mouth to mimic my actions. He welcomes my fingers into his luscious mouth, one at a time; kissing them, pulling them into the warm moisture. My body tingles when he rolls his tongue around my fingertips the way he does my clit when he buries his lips between my thighs!

Every Lady is a Woman,
but Every Woman is NOT a Lady

Our quiet game of mirrored actions plays out with him willingly watching as I slip my fingers into my hot moisture, slide them in and out, then insert them into my own mouth, licking, sucking, and tasting my unique nectar. The thirst in his eyes makes my pussy wet, as he knows he is next, but not until I say so...

Now that I have his complete attention, I part my juicy lips, slowly roll my finger around my growing clit before inserting three of my small fingers into the pulsating dampness, withdraw them, and run them down the length of my tongue.

My companion's breathing is heavier, his eyes filled with longing, his manhood is pronounced with need. I take my place in front of him on the floor between his naked thighs, my back to his chest, and let my thighs fall apart. His erection stabs at my round ass, but it's not time yet; he hasn't repeated my action yet. Taking his left hand, I cup it to my breast, surrendering control to him as he gently squeezes my nipple between his fingers and thumb.

"Ummm, yeah Baby. Just like that..."

I take his right hand and bring it down my body until I have three of his fingers shoved deep into me. I lose myself, guiding them up and down from my pearl to my sopping Pretty Girl until I burst all over them! I delight in watching him lick the juices from his fingers exactly as I did. We exchange quick knowing glances and he understands permission is granted! He holds my gaze as he ushers me forward while he strokes his piece and bends me over. Grasping my hips, he delivers himself into me, pounding into my sweet pussy from the back. I throw my ass back to him, taking every inch of his dick until my Pretty Girl is engorged and popping! My lover fucks me deep, slow stroking until he groans and shoots off a much awaited load while I rock out the last of my orgasms on his pulsating piece. My naughty

Every Lady is a Woman,
but Every Woman is NOT a Lady

little beast is a delighted specimen, having arrived at this

tingling happy place following some finger licking fun!

Essence K. Berry

Every Lady is a Woman,
but Every Woman is NOT a Lady

Lesson #10: "A lady is careful to conceal her undergarments"

Part One: The Observation

Blue Jean Friday at the office! I look so forward to the days when I can toss my business casual attire aside for the comfort of my jeans. It is often the highlight of my work week. This particular Friday, I've selected my jet black pair; the ones that hug my womanly curves in all the right places, stretching where I need them to stretch, snug where I like them! Since I am sporting a red blouse today, of course my panties and bra are red as well. One thing I insist on is my outer wear matching my underwear! My sweetie adores that about me. He frequently allows his imagination to soar each time he lays eyes on me. He has an intimate relationship with each pair of low riders, high cut, thong, boy shorts, and barely-there panties I own. That man can close his eyes and picture every lacy, front hook, satin and lace push-up bra in my drawer of goodies.

Essence K. Berry

Every Lady is a Woman, but Every Woman is NOT a Lady

To add to my compulsion, he ensures I not only have the lotions I love, but the luscious body washes to match each one as well! It turns him on when he watches me prepare for my day. My sweet scent lingers throughout the house following my showers, tempting his sense of smell. He enjoys the slow application of the creamy body butter as I perform my daily ritual just for him. I usually apply it with exaggerated intent. He is thrilled as I touch myself, especially when I forbid him to reciprocate. It's a little game we play. He is forbidden to touch my body, nor his own, but he is allowed to watch and give verbal instruction. He is compliant and so willing to partake in our games of control.

On this particular Friday, I am feeling relaxed at the end of my day, as there are only two of us remaining in the office; myself and one female co-worker. I am usually very stringent about my attire, ensuring I am presentable at all times, especially in mixed company. I

Every Lady is a Woman, but Every Woman is NOT a Lady

believe a woman can be sexy without revealing all. Keep them guessing is my philosophy. However, it is late, I'm relaxed, and I have been in and out of my chair all evening retrieving materials. In my current state, I fail to make the usual provisions to cover my ample backside when my tunic rides up from the friction of my movements. This indiscretion reveals the top of my panties. I know this woman; I am comfortable with her. It's no big deal between two girls if a little skin is exposed. Right?

WRONG! This is obviously NOT the case tonight! I've noticed in the past hour or so how pronounced my co-worker's nipples are when she stops to make an inquiry at my desk. It's almost on the verge of indecent! Her breasts are much larger than my full perky tits, so of course the pronounced exposure of her nipples draw my attention, as they remind me of soft miniature marshmellows; swollen and punching against her tight sweater. After several unnecessary trips past my desk, she finally stops to drop a huge shocker in my lap.

"Girl, you are wearing those jeans today! I've watched you all day and I had to tell you that before we leave here tonight. It's been a pleasure!"

"Ummm, the pleasure is all mine? Do I say thank you?" I fumble like a blubbering idiot. What was I supposed to do with that?!

"Have I embarrassed you? I don't mean any disrespect; I know you have a man. It's just that I have admired the shape of your ass, those round thighs, that pigeon toed walk! It's sexy!"

Again, I meet her with the blank stare as I process what is unfolding before me...

"Don't get me wrong, I love men! Give me a big thick dick any day! But you are a beautiful woman. Look at how your titties sit up! You don't think much of bending over at your desk in a room full of women. Why would you? But when I'm working at the desk behind you and you bend over, especially with those jeans on, I can see everything, including your lips! You just have a raw sex appeal and it's like you don't even know it!"

I watch her full bright red lips move and observe the excited twinkle in her eye in astonishment.

"You've been *watching* me? For how long?

My co-worker closes the space between us, placing her body right next to my chair so her hip grazes my arm.

Inhaling deeply, she gushes in a low tone, "You always smell delicious too. That's why that man calls and visits every chance he gets. Girl he knows..."

"Hold on. Knows what?" Still attempting to process this crazy scene, I follow her bold gaze as it travels my body.

Every Lady is a Woman, but Every Woman is NOT a Lady

In a low lusty voice, she practically purrs, "He knows your pussy is good. It's juicy too, isn't it? Fat ass lips!"

My mind is blown! What the FUCK?!?!

"Girl I don't mean any harm. I was sitting back there and saw the red lace from these panties and got a peek at that red bra strap. Shit! It was turning me on! I have those same panties at home. They're all lace, right? The boy shorts that showcase your cheeks?"

She is rapidly beckoning my beast to attention! However, the lady in me is putting up a good fight! *Don't you dare respond to her! You are a lady dammit!* I try so hard to keep the lady at the surface, but it is becoming increasingly difficult to maintain!

Ignoring the proper little scolding voice in my head, I spring into action, unlocking the chains, eagerly freeing the beast!

Every Lady is a Woman,
but Every Woman is NOT a Lady

"Yes ma'am! Those would be the ones! However, I'll never wear them with denim again! The seam of these jeans have created friction against the lace and I've been creamy all day!"

"Oh my gosh! I know! I learned that lesson the hard way! Can I see?!"

Without confirmation or permission, she lifts my shirt tail, runs her slender fingers across the inside of my jeans, feeling my lace covered ass. To my surprise, she then asks if the bra is all lace as well, quickly taking a chance to pull out the top of my blouse to help herself to a quick peek down the front!

"Seriously?! SERIOUSLY? Did you get a good look?!"

"I really didn't get a *good* look. Would you let me see more?"

"My man would have a FIT!"

Essence K. Berry

Of course that doesn't deter my curiosity. "What would you like to see *exactly*?"

I watch her hands travel over her own juicy bosom as she contemplates the possibilities. My co-worker almost sounds giddy as she starts to exclaim, "Ooh! I want to see your titties, that bodacious ass, hell, I want to see it all! If he is willing, I would love to see him too!"

Now she has my complete attention! "You want to see him too? You know I'm not going to have sex with you. And he would *die* before he invited a third into bed with us! So how do you propose we do this?"

I lean back in the chair, doing an intentional slow caress of my thighs, sliding my hands up, stopping just short of the mound of my Pretty Girl. I can feel the warmth through the tight material that parts my thick lips.

Every Lady is a Woman,
but Every Woman is NOT a Lady

She watches, hands roaming over her own shapely hips and round ass.

"Hell, I don't know girl! Make a video, take some pictures! Just let me see the goods!"

"That's not a bad idea! You want to watch him suck my titties?" I ask as I lightly rub my hands across my nipples, cupping my full breasts.

"Yes! I want to see him lick 'em, suck 'em, stuff 'em in his mouth, hard, soft, all of that!"

Staring into her face, locking in on her full mouth, I inquire further, "Would you like to see him rub his dick across my lips? I love head and he likes to watch me swallow his meat."

"Yes. Yes! All of that shit! When?!"

Pulling my gaze from hers, I swivel my chair, retrieve my phone from its cradle, and punch in a series of numbers. When I am greeted by the familiar, "Hey Baby", I face her, allow my gaze to burn through her, and speak my commands into the phone. "Hey Baby. When I get off, I need you at my place, camera charged, and make sure your bush is trimmed. Tell me what I just said." I continue to slice my stare through her....

"Charge the camera, shave my man, beat you to the house!"

"Cool Babe. See you in two hours. Love you!"

"Love you too Baby!"

My co-worker watches the scene unfold and her jaw dropping response has me elated!

"Just like that?!"

"Yes ma'am, just like that; I love that about him. He is up for anything. He stopped asking questions a long time ago. He learned quickly whatever I ask of him, he should just do it because he will enjoy it as much as I do."

"Okay, just make sure I get to see you in these panties and this bra. Let me see it all! I want to see whatever you are willing to show me! Oh! I can watch it over and over and play by myself! Ooo shit! I'm excited girl! Do you guys have sex tapes?"

"Not yet. He has photographed me, but this will be our first video."

"Great! I look forward to it! So glad I finally said something! See what sweet treats I get!"

Every Lady is a Woman,
but Every Woman is NOT a Lady

Part Two: Lights, Camera, Action

As soon as I pull up, I see him under the beam of my porch light. He is beaming so bright he could light up the night! Walking up to greet him, I reach for his already pronounced manhood and stroke him through his pants while I connect my lips to his full mouth. When my sweetie gets hard his pants barely contain his mammoth meat.

"Come in and take your place in The Seat of Honor. I'll join you shortly."

Taking my leave from him, I treat myself to a quick shower, followed by a generous application of matching body butter, massaging it into my skin until it appears to glow. I step into a pair of black lace and satin boy shorts and an all lace matching black bra that compliments beautifully. No make-up is required. My skin is glowing like a dream. I forfeit additional perfume as well, since my aroma already fills the house. Besides, it's *me* I want him to taste and smell later when his mouth devours my body. Checking my reflection from every angle, I am extremely pleased!

The view from the back reveals the curve of my back, the lift of my ass, and divulges the cheeks of a juicy peach, while exposing gorgeous full hips and my sweet round thighs. The front view makes me wet just taking it all in! My breasts are high plump melons! The material reveals a full view of my tasty treats through the lace, yielding the sight of my nipples pressing against the restraints of the thin lace! My Pretty Girl is a smooth delicious strawberry, showcasing the swell of my lips, though tastefully concealed by the gorgeous material. I am the picture of sweet fruit, ripe for the picking. It's all perfectly astounding! I'm ready for my close up!

My sweetie is still obediently glued to The Throne where I told him to stay. His mouth gapes as I approach his seat of honor. He takes the sight of me in, inch by sweet glossy inch.

"Are you ready Babe? I'm gonna make you a star!"

I get a slow head nod from him before my words sink into that sweet bald head of his. Comprehension clouds his face. "A star? What exactly did you say we were doing?"

Ignoring his inquiry and removing one of the overstuffed pillows from my sofa, I place it on the floor between his feet. He watches while I position myself between his knees, instructing him to turn the camera on. Doing exactly as he is coached without further inquiry, he gets comfortable, forgets he was asking me a question, and prepares to let his light shine!

I take time to pull him forward first, sucking his full bottom lip, allowing my taught tits to caress his crotch. Satisfied when his protrusion threatens to escape the material that is now stretched to the limit, I know he is ready to begin.

My tongue dances with his; into his warm mouth, across his lips, and back into the inviting moisture that beckons for more. Rubbing him through his pants until he moans into my mouth and squirms against my hand, I have no doubt my sweetie is ready for action!

Relaxing again, I sit up, my bottom resting on my heels, and I gladly free his anxious erection. I'm excited as I get up close and personal with his throbbing pole! He is viewing the scene unfolding before him via the lens of the camera he holds. His head is thick, the veins running trails up and down the shaft are strong, and the color is even and beautiful!

My mate's girth is unbelievable! As I close in the space between my mouth and his gorgeous piece, I am met with a dazzling involuntary flex by his flawless muscle! I slowly draw my gaze from his wondrous masterpiece, fix my gaze on the camera's eye, lick my lips, then run my fingers slowly across my begging nipples, and speak the truth into the lens, "Sucking your dick makes my pussy sooo wet!"

With that confession, I spread my knees, slide my hand into my panties, finger my juicy pussy, and wrap my sticky fingers around his mammoth dick. My co-star begins to whisper to me as I kiss his lovely head, "Take your time baby. Ooo shit, take your time."

I slide my hand, coated with my own honey, up and down his glorious shaft, opening my mouth over his head, just enough to moisten the tip. "Those lips. Shit! Ease down on it baby. A little at a time..."

I am careful to move slowly as I kiss the tip, eyes cast down, concentrating, working on him. I tongue kiss his opening, sucking, kissing, and rolling my tongue around the head, taking him further in on each rotation around his massive tip.

Every Lady is a Woman,
but Every Woman is NOT a Lady

Just when his legs tense, I look straight into the camera and pointedly instruct him, "Give it back to me", before I drop my jaw and plunge him deep into my throat!

I continue to look into the eye of the camera as my mouth consumes him, wetting his sweet meat, gliding up and down on it, meeting the gentle thrust of his hips.

"Ummm hmmm." He is wet from my saliva, penetrating the depths of my throat. I suck him in deep, blow him out, caressing his full sack, massaging up and down his healthy erection with my small hands. My pussy is throbbing at the tantalizing taste of my juices on his sweet meat.

"More!" I encourage from around his pulsating erection. He responds with deeper thrusts. Holding him steady in my hand, I submit to his oral penetration, returning the blow job of his life! My Pretty Girl drizzles with each moan he releases to the rhythm of my head bob. I squeeze my breasts, take his dick, and pat my thick pus through the lace panties.

My hands dwarf in comparison to his colossal manhood. I seize his erection with both hands, trail several kisses around the head of his stiff prick, lick him from the base of his shaft up to the tip, and drop my gaping mouth over the head again. Holding him with both hands because he jumps on each down stroke, I work the moisture from my mouth up and down his massive piece with my hands while I bob up and down on his thickness.

My head dips, his legs quiver, and periodically I have to admonish him to hold the camera steady. I look into the camera occasionally to make contact with him, but more so to acknowledge her, as I know she will be watching the scene unfold soon. It turns me on to know she can stop, rewind, and take in the events of the night, as I satisfy him and allow her to view our bodies as she touches her own. I moan as I take him in, slurping down and wrapping my tongue around his veined shaft as I suck hard on the way back up. I blow and I suck until the quaking of his legs becomes too much to ignore.

The camera continues to slip and slide as my sweetie is enthralled by the act being performed on him.

"Damn, this shit looks crazy from here! It's unreal!" He continues his voyeur from the camera's eye. "Suck me baby! Slow it down, slow down and take it in real slow. Just like that. Yeah, shit! Oooh that shit looks goood!"

I look right at the camera, as if she is right there watching, close up, holding my head and guiding my mouth down on his dick while she touches her hot pussy.

"You like that?" I kiss the tip...

"You want more Baby?" I jack him off while I swallow his balls and hummm....

"Mmm, you feel so good, taste so good!" I rub his wet piece all over my face, kissing it each time it passes my mouth. Over my face, my neck, down my chest to the swell of my bursting melons, waiting to erupt out of the thin material that barely contains them.

"Shit Baby, rub it over those nipples."

I comply, caressing my ample tits, squeezing my nipples, and stroking them until I coax them to the bra's edge. He holds his dick with one hand and the camera with the other so I can suck him while I unsnap my bra, freeing my juicy fruit in one motion. I suck up to his head with a "POP", smile, and wink at the camera!

"That was a bonus for you Baby!"

Relieving Baby's erection from his hand, I place it between my voluminous mounds and go to work on him! I massage him with my tits, moving them up and down the shaft while I slurp him hard and wet down my throat.

Every Lady is a Woman, but Every Woman is NOT a Lady

"Fuck my mouth Baby. Work those hips! Damn I'm hot!"

He gives more, moaning while warm saliva drops down my hands, drizzling onto my naked breasts.

"Baby you are so good! I want to bust in that pussy!" I stroke him with my mouth again… "I know that pussy is hot!" I suck him in as deep as I can take him into my throat…"Turn around and bend over so I can see it! Shit that feels good!" He watches me take his head and squeeze him between my abundant breasts… "Damn baby you have to come off of it! I'm about to blow! Gimme that fat pussy! Shit!"

One more thrust and he pulls down, hoping to free himself from my grasp.

"Ok Baby, but bring that with you! She wants to see it all! Come on so she can watch you get in this pussy!"

We literally race to the bedroom, where we

attempt to find a suitable place for the camera!

"Just hold it! Hold it and fuck me now! NOW! My pussy is hot!"

"Sucking my dick does that for you?"

I meet his gaze before I assume his favorite position, assuring him he can have it exactly like wants it. "Mmm hmmm!" I post up on my knees for him and bend over, exposing my wetness to him; the wetness he created when he slid in and out of my mouth!

He holds the camera long enough to penetrate my wet opening. I push back with the hunger of a deprived woman! I rock on his stiff meat, dip down and bring it back for him. I roll my hips, take him in deeper, and fuck him while he observes through the camera's lens.

"This is all yours! Fuck this dick! Work on it Baby! Work on it!!"

I give it to him harder, rotating my hips and popping my pussy on his fabulous rock!

Every Lady is a Woman,
but Every Woman is NOT a Lady

"Stand up in this pussy! I need you to fuck me Baby! Beat this pussy up!"

He finally drops the camera on the bed beside me so he can grasp my hips and pull me closer to the edge of the bed! Pounding into my eager wetness, he delivers long strokes that force me to surrender to his will! I know he will drive us home!

I spread my knees more, perched on the bed's edge, and grasp the sheets into my small fits. I am prepared for the ride!

He digs his strong fingers into the fronts of my thighs as his speed increases to match my rocking motion. Leaning slightly back so my ass rests on the front of his thighs, he supports me while I bounce on his dick.

"That's right Baby! Ride this dick! Get that shit! You want her to see you ride this dick like this? Huh?" He pounds harder! "Look at that ass! Damn you are *soaked*! Gimme this fat pussy!"

He digs deeper into my thighs and I bounce faster, holding my tits, squeezing my nipples when I feel the familiar tingle spread through my hot body!

"Knowing she is watching turns you on doesn't it?! Doesn't it?! You like that shit Baby? You like being watched?"

"Yes! I do! This is good! Yes! I do! Yes!"

"Baby get that nut! Fuck this dick!" He growls in my ear as he reaches forward and pulls me into a full upright position, taking my big titties into his rough grasp!

I drop my knees apart and squeeze my muscle on his muscle, caressing him when I clench my ass and stroke him down. I work myself into a cum induced frenzy; grinding on his monster sized muscle, whispering to him about how she is watching and I'll bet she is coming with us!

Every Lady is a Woman,
but Every Woman is NOT a Lady

The thought of him in my mouth, his pole between my tits, and fucking me deep while she watches brings me to a series of immeasurable orgasms that rip through my body! I attempt to resume my position on all fours, but his hands hinder me, as he catches me on the way down.

"Not yet my love. Ride this dick til you get the last drop! Ride it slow. Keep squeezing on me just like that. Yeah, just like that, ooh yeah! Fuuuccckkk! Work that ass!"

With that, he grabs my throat with his strong hand, squeezing with a steady grip as I do a slow wind on his dick. He squeezes, I rock, and his other hand pushes my hips down harder on his pulsating piece!

Grunts and growls announce his arrival and satisfaction. Before he releases his hold on my throat, I turn my head and kiss his full lips deeply.

"This is why I love you. My baby is always

ready!"

"What the hell do you women do at work when no one is there? On second thought, don't tell me; I may not want to know!"

Needless to say the botched attempt at amateur porn never left our hands. The footage of the blow job was extraordinary and an excellent learning tool! We watched it several more times and fucked brazenly to it! The animalistic sounds from the bedroom scene alone delivered him deep into my every time we watched it! Real sexual noises turn us both on! We never shared the video, opting to use it for our entertainment only! I shared the details with my coworker and she was content with those, stating she could get a mental pic and tucked the details away for later.

If my sweetie only knew, this all started because I got caught with my panties showing! Such an unladylike blunder, but a hell of a price to pay!

*Every Lady is a Woman,
but Every Woman is NOT a Lady*

Advice from the Old School:

Your clothes do not have to be two sizes too small to get the attention of the man across the hall. Sexy is a state of mind; an attitude. Find your sexy and let it shine!

A woman can get sex before she can get a meal! You can extend your arm and strike a man who is willing to have sex with you. Sexual companionship comes a dime a dozen. YOU are in control of your outcome. Choose wisely!

A little can go a long way. A lady doesn't have to be seen, heard, or smelled from a mile away to gain recognition. Do all things in moderation. He will notice…

Quality is better than quantity. It is fine to attract many men; however be selective when you choose a quality man. You will know the difference.

*Every Lady is a Woman,
but Every Woman is NOT a Lady*

A real woman knows her worth! Know who you are and what is important to you. Never settle! Don't do a thing to please the next person. Do what you do because it pleases YOU!

Make him work for it! Any good thing worth having its worth waiting for.

Be a lady in the streets and a beast in the sheets. Train your beast. Let her out to play when it's appropriate! Unleash her when it is not detrimental to your public persona. Be the lady, but let your little monster out to stretch her legs and feed her appetite.

Save a little something for later. If you are into him, introduce him to the lady first. Let him meet your beast a little at a time. Flirt with him; tease him a little. Let him meet your wild side when he deserves it!

Every Lady is a Woman,
but Every Woman is NOT a Lady

Ladies can have fun too! Allow the lady to attract the gentleman. Make sure he can entertain you as well as please you. Chivalry is not dead ladies! Let him hold your door! This affords him the view of the goods he will get later (if you choose to give him the cookies) while he treats you like the lady you are!

When you get him behind closed doors (or on the picnic table, the front porch, or in the garage) have fun! Let your hair down, tell him what you want, and enjoy yourself! Ladies have orgasms too!

Epilogue

I was seemingly clueless to my actions and mannerisms and the effects they appeared to have on the opposite sex in my post teen years. Although I have always been a very intelligent woman, I was sorely naive to the obvious.

My flighty "do what feels good to me" mantra appealed to me, even then. I never paid heed to being in close proximity to another during conversation; I am comfortable being a space invader, in spite of my teachings to the contrary.

I am a hugger, disregarding the full lift of my breasts and the effect they have on the recipient. It is natural for me to touch another individual during conversation; what can I say, I'm a touchy feely kinda girl. The world around me says it's against the rules, but I like human contact.

Every Lady is a Woman, but Every Woman is NOT a Lady

During face to face conversations, I never tried to mask my appreciation for the cut of a man's jaw; my excitement of the length of a set of sexy lashes; or my appeal for the full curve of a pair of sensuous lips. Of course it is deemed callous for a woman to be so unabashed, but is it a crime to appreciate a naturally beautiful being?

I was even bold enough to unapologetically allow my eyes to travel seductively over another's gorgeous features while onlookers observed. I have a healthy love of the human body and I'm not ashamed of that. Although the desire has always been alive in me, I was not always as receptive as I should have been to other's observation of the same little things in me. Hence, the lessons of my distracted mannerisms and disregard of the admonishment from my elders resulted in me getting fucked practicality every time I tossed aside my ladylike teachings. Was it worth it? Of course it was! I could

Every Lady is a Woman,
but Every Woman is NOT a Lady

have walked a straight, narrow path, but the road less traveled yielded more adventure! So are the tales of a lady and the insatiable beast she submits to…

Printed in Great Britain
by Amazon